PUFFIN BOOKS

Computer for Charlie

When Dad's computer program is erased, Charlie gets the blame and nearly misses summer camp. To forget his troubles, he enters the school computer competition. Meanwhile, the real culprit is found and to make things up to Charlie there's a special surprise in store!

In the second story, Charlie and his friends enjoy summer camp. Charlie loves football and is desperate to be chosen for the County Rovers, but Bob Sharp stops at nothing to keep Charlie out of the team.

These two lively and amusing stories appear together in one volume for the first time.

Joy Allen studied music at college and gained her L.R.A.M. She went on to become an infant teacher and now teaches piano. She has three children and five grandchildren, and lives in Rutland with her husband.

Other books by Joy Allen

Cup Final for Charlie
Stick To It, Charlie

Joy Allen

Computer for Charlie

Illustrated by Thelma Lambert

Puffin Books

PUFFIN BOOKS

Published by the Penguin Group
Penguin Books Ltd, 27 Wrights Lane, London W8 5TZ, England
Penguin Books USA Inc., 375 Hudson Street, New York, New York 10014, USA
Penguin Books Australia Ltd, Ringwood, Victoria, Australia
Penguin Books Canada Ltd, 10 Alcorn Avenue, Toronto, Ontario, Canada M4V 3B2
Penguin Books (NZ) Ltd, 182–190 Wairau Road, Auckland 10, New Zealand

Penguin Books Ltd, Registered Offices: Harmondsworth, Middlesex, England

Computer for Charlie first published by Hamish Hamilton 1987
County Rovers for Charlie first published by Hamish Hamilton 1988
Published in one volume in Puffin Books 1990
10 9 8 7

Printed in England by Clays Ltd, St Ives plc
Filmset in Monophoto Photina

Contents

COMPUTER FOR CHARLIE

Chapter One

'Don't touch!' Dad shouted.

'But – Dad – !'

'I mean what I say!' Dad looked flustered and buried his head deeper in the instruction book.

'We have computers at school and I know how to work them,' Charlie insisted.

Dad looked up, scowling.

'This has been programmed for my

office work. An expert from London came especially to set it up.'

Dad studied the keyboard, desperately trying to remember which key he was supposed to press.

'Not much use if you don't know how to call it up,' observed Charlie smugly.

'CHARLIE! For heaven's sake, stop hovering round! Please go away. I have to work this out for myself. I shall be thankful when you go to summer camp.'

Charlie wandered into the kitchen.

Mike was cleaning his football boots using Mum's best kitchen knife. He was gleefully scooping out lumps of dried mud and flicking them on to a newspaper.

'Cor! Dad won't be too pleased. That's today's paper!'

Charlie ducked as Mike hurled a piece of mud in his direction. It hit Sheeba, the cat, instead. She looked very affronted and leapt on to the draining board where Mum was washing Josie's hair at the sink.

Charlie retrieved the mud and threw it back at Mike. It hit him on the ear.

'OUCH!' Mike cried. 'That hurt!'

'Stop that, Charlie!' Mum snapped.

'Mike started it!' Charlie complained. 'I always get the blame.'

Mum didn't reply. She was too busy rinsing the soap from Josie's hair. Sheeba curled up on the window-sill. Her nose twitched every time a bubble floated her way.

'Dad's terribly bad-tempered now he's got his computer. He won't let me help at all,' Charlie grumbled. 'I wish it was

next Saturday. I can't wait for summer camp. Mr Taylor, the new football coach, is going to be in charge. He's talent-spotting for the Junior County Team.'

'Not the Junior Rovers?' Mike gasped as Charlie nodded. 'Cor! Lucky thing, Charlie. You might get chosen with a bit of luck.'

'You've only four more days at school until the end of term,' Mum reminded Charlie. 'The time will fly.'

'As it's the last week, we're going to be allowed to use the computers when we want. In fact, there's to be a computer "write a story" competition. Great! After football, I like computers best. I wish Dad would let me have a go on his.'

'Nobody can help him,' Mike sighed.

‘I will! I will!’ Josie cried in a muffled voice. She was holding a flannel at her face to stop the soap getting in her eyes.

Suddenly Dad stormed through the kitchen.

‘That machine is driving me crazy!’ he fumed. ‘I’ll do some digging in the garden before it rains.’

There was a brief period of peace, broken by a bang on the back door. Charlie went to see who it was and came back in a second.

‘It’s Joe! Can I play football with the gang? I’ll just go and change into my old trousers.’

He didn’t wait for a reply.

‘Don’t be late for lunch!’ Mum shouted as he jumped the stairs two at a time.

She wrapped Josie's hair in a towel and lifted her down.

'All rinsed and clean! Run off and watch *Saturday Special* on the telly until I have time to fetch the hair-drier.'

Josie wandered into the dining-room. Dad's computer was still on. The screen was full of words and numbers and

looked very boring. No wonder he got fed up with it! Charlie had told her that they played super games on the ones they had at school.

She pressed a few keys to see if she could make it more fun. One of the keys said 'CAN' so she tried that but it only made the writing disappear.

She could read 'OFF' so she tried that – it made the screen black. Then she felt rather frightened in case Dad was angry.

Jumping down the step that led to the sitting-room, she switched on the TV set.

'MICKEY MOUSE!' she cried. 'That's much better!'

Charlie clattered down the stairs and Josie heard the front door slam.

Then she saw the gang run past the window on their way to the park.

Chapter Two

'Let's go!' Charlie yelled.

He headed the ball to Joe, who dribbled it to Titch. He gave a little kick ahead but Mac intercepted.

'Pass to me!' shouted Tony, roaring down the field with Mac at his side. Jason raced into goal to defend. His heart pumped with excitement. Nearer and nearer they came, running like the wind. THUMP! Tony booted the ball with all his might. It soared high and Jason leapt in the air, catching it firmly.

The others panted up and thumped him on the back.

'GREAT SAVE!' they cried. 'Good as Peter Shilton!'

'Dad thinks it's sissy when footballers hug each other,' laughed Jake. 'That's why you're getting a thump instead!'

'I bet Mr Taylor notices you at the summer camp,' Charlie said.

'I'm sure you'll be chosen for the county team,' replied Jason. 'You're brilliant at shooting.'

'Let's all practise shooting at Jason,' suggested Joe. 'Like we do at school.'

Jason felt quite dizzy by the time they'd finished.

'Who wants a turn at goalkeeper?' he gasped.

'I'll be first!' cried Titch. 'Perhaps the jumping will make me grow taller!'

Titch was surprisingly good in goal, but soon it began to rain steadily and Charlie looked at his watch.

'It's nearly one o'clock!' he exclaimed. 'Dad's in a bad mood and I mustn't be late for lunch.'

'My Dad is always cross on a Saturday morning. He can never get the mower started,' Tony sighed. 'And Mum goes

about with a long face if he hasn't mown the grass before he watches the sport on telly.'

'Race you home!' Charlie was off like a thunderbolt and didn't stop until he rushed into the kitchen.

'Super game!' he announced.

There was something wrong. Charlie looked round the room. Dad, Mike and

Josie were sitting like statues at the table. The only sound was the hissing and spitting of the sausages Mum was cooking.

Pushing back his chair, Dad rose to his feet.

He looked furious!

Sheeba scuttled under the table and Josie began to cry.

'Come with me, Charlie!'

Dad led him to the computer.

'I told you not to touch this!'

'But . . . Dad . . . I never . . .!' Charlie began to tremble.

Dad wouldn't listen.

'You have ruined the whole program. It has disappeared. Gone for ever.'

'But, Dad . . . I didn't . . .' Charlie tried again to explain.

'I could even lose my job.'

Charlie felt dreadful. His eyes pricked and his throat felt tight.

'I didn't touch it!' he shouted. 'I always get the blame for everything. It must have been somebody else.'

Charlie ran upstairs to his room and flung himself on the bed.

Dad followed him.

'You deliberately disobeyed me and will have to be punished,' he said quietly. 'You won't be going to the summer school camp.'

Chapter Three

'Summer school camp won't be the same without you,' sighed Joe.

'I think I'll run away!' Charlie said desperately. 'Perhaps it will make Dad change his mind.'

'It might make him madder,' Joe warned. 'You'd get cold and hungry. It wouldn't be much fun, I'm sure!'

'But I didn't touch his silly old computer,' wailed Charlie. 'He probably lost the program himself, by mistake . . . or . . . perhaps?'

Charlie paused and thought carefully.

'Perhaps what?' Joe asked impatiently.

'I was wondering if Josie played with it. But . . . no – Mum was washing her hair at the time.'

All the gang were miserable because Charlie wasn't going to be allowed to go to the summer school camp. Mac lent him his new bike and Tony let him have a go with his racing roller-skates. Nothing made Charlie feel any better.

'Computer time!' Titch cried as the school bell rang. 'Let's play "Bat 'n' Ball",

it's one of your favourite games, Charlie. Then we can have a go with "Satellite Warrior", and "Atom Smasher".'

'I like "Dragons" best,' Mac said. 'I scored loads of points last time by killing dragons.'

'I don't want to play,' Charlie murmured. 'I have to write my story for the competition.'

'You can do that later,' insisted Mac. 'Anyway, Steve Oddy is bound to win. He's such a brainy swot, he always wins everything.'

'He won't this time, because I'm going to try my very hardest.'

'Good for you!' Joe said admiringly. 'Don't forget, Mr Kerry says you have to make sure three words come into the story.'

'WITCH! SHAMPOO! CAVE!' Titch shouted helpfully.

'Cor! I wouldn't know where to begin!' Tony gasped.

'I like writing stories,' shrugged Charlie. 'You just use your imagination.'

'Oh! Come on, Charlie! Let's play computer games. Our names are down for today's dinner break and we mustn't miss our chance.'

The gang heaved Charlie to his feet and pushed him into the computer room. They rushed for the software box to choose the discs.

'I think computers are super!' Tony cried. 'Not only can you play games on them, but you can use them for the sums and writing problems we do in Mr Kerry's class. Mr Kerry's great too!'

'I like typing words on the keyboard,'

Joe said. 'Next term we're learning how to make our own programs.'

'We send messages to each other,' Tony boasted. 'I sent a message to Jake which said, "You are a silly nit". Suddenly, Mr Kerry came round to see what we were doing. He didn't like it at all. "LEAVE THE ROOM AT ONCE!" he shouted.'

Charlie felt better when he kept beating Titch at 'Bat 'n' Ball'. Then he remembered he wouldn't be with them all at summer camp, and a depressing black cloud seemed to hang over him.

'I'll miss my talent being spotted,' he confided in Joe. 'I'll never have a chance to play for the Junior Rovers County Team.'

'Cheer up, Charlie!' Joe sympathized. 'Perhaps you'll win the "write a story" competition.'

'I'm going to write my story now,' Charlie said. 'I can stay after school and print it out.'

'Steve Oddy has already done his,' sighed Joe. 'It has to be in first thing tomorrow.'

Charlie's stomach gave a lurch. He desperately wanted to win. Even though he wasn't to blame for touching Dad's computer, it might make him less angry. Dad might even be proud of him. He must write the best story!

That afternoon, Mr Kerry allowed Charlie to work in the library. The others were busy tidying cupboards and desks.

Mr Kerry popped in to see how he was getting on.

'May I stay after school to use the

word processor to print out my story?' asked Charlie.

'Of course,' replied Mr Kerry. 'I'll ask Mike to let your mother know you'll be late home.'

Joe came in to bring some books back to the library.

'Have you managed to fit in witch, shampoo and cave?' he whispered. 'Let's hear it!'

'I'm not going to read you my story now,' Charlie said. 'Mr Kerry says the best ones will be read out on the last day of term.'

'Oh, go on, Charlie!' Joe pleaded. 'Be a sport!'

'Certainly not!' Charlie laughed. 'But I'll tell you the gist of it.'

'Can I listen as well?' Tony appeared in the doorway.

Charlie nodded, then began.

'Mrs Trip has a daughter, Jenny, who doesn't always tell the truth. Mrs Trip seeks advice from a witch who lives in a cave in the middle of a spooky wood. The witch gives Mrs Trip a bottle of magic shampoo to use on Jenny's hair. Every time Jenny tells a lie, her hair turns bright green! That soon does the trick!'

'Poor Jenny!' Joe chuckled. 'It's a jolly good story, Charlie.'

'I've just read Steve Oddy's!' Tony looked guilty. 'Mr Kerry left it lying around on his desk.'

'What's his about?' Charlie asked anxiously.

'Well – er – let me think.' Tony scratched his head. 'It's about a boy called Peter. He has a big bald patch on his head. He goes to a witch who gives him a bottle of shampoo, but it's not shampoo!'

'What do you mean?' Joe looked puzzled.

'Well – the bottle label says "GROWS ANYWHERE" and the witch thinks it's shampoo and will grow hair.'

'What happens?' asked Charlie.

'Peter uses the contents of the bottle on his head. The next morning, he looks in the mirror and, to his horror, his head is covered with mustard and cress!'

Charlie and Joe fell about laughing.

'Shut up, you two! Let me finish!' Tony began to laugh as well. 'He has to wear a woolly cap until the mustard and cress withers away.'

'So he's still left with the bald patch,' finished Charlie. 'That's not a very good ending.'

'It's funnier than yours, though,' Tony remarked thoughtlessly.

Charlie's stomach did a somersault.

'Clear off, now!' Charlie looked flustered. 'You're putting me off.'

It was quite late by the time Charlie had finished. Mr Kerry was still in the classroom and Charlie handed him the story.

'I'm sorry you won't be with us at summer camp,' said Mr Kerry.

'I'm sorry, too,' he replied sadly.

Charlie gulped. He didn't try to explain, and the black cloud hung over him again.

It was worse at home. Mike tried to be especially nice to him, which somehow made Charlie behave badly towards him. He missed Mike throwing the dishcloth at him and having fights together. They were only friendly fights really and good fun.

Charlie overheard Mike tell Mum that he felt sorry for Charlie.

'You get on my wick!' Charlie shouted. 'Why don't you shut up and mind your own business!'

Just at that moment Uncle Tim appeared.

'What's the matter, Charlie?' he asked. 'It's not like you to speak like that.'

'Dad thinks I tampered with his new computer,' he explained. 'But I didn't touch it! I didn't! Truly!'

'Who was it, then?' Uncle Tim looked perplexed.

'I don't know!' Charlie cried. 'But Dad won't let me go to summer camp!'

Dad appeared from nowhere.

'It must have been you, Charlie! There's no one else it could have been.'

Josie, who was helping Mum lay the table, suddenly went very red.

'Josie?' Mum paused. 'I wonder – Have you ever touched Dad's computer?'

Josie burst into tears.

'Daddy was cross!' she sobbed. 'I was frightened!'

'Oh dear!' Dad looked shocked. 'I am so sorry, Charlie. I never dreamed it could be Josie. It's all my fault. Of course, you shall go to camp.'

He hugged Josie.

'Don't cry, love! Everything is going to be all right. I'm going on a course to learn about computers; then I can show the others at work how to use them. I'm afraid I've been rather like a growly, cross old bear just lately!'

'WHOOPEE!' Charlie gasped. 'Perhaps I'll still have a chance to play for the Rovers!'

'And I think you will be chosen,' Dad laughed. 'Mr Kerry told me you booted the ball like a professional.'

'I'll have to decide whether to be a

footballer or a computer expert when I leave school!'

Uncle Tim smiled. He had suddenly made a decision himself. He had been wondering what to buy Charlie for his birthday. It could be a combined Christmas present.

The last day of term soon arrived. There was a buzz of excitement as Mr Kerry walked on to the platform to take assembly.

After wishing them all a happy holiday, he said: 'I shall now announce the winner of the "write a story" competition. I am awarding first prize to CHARLIE LAVENDER, with Steve Oddy as a close runner-up. I am giving Charlie the prize because his story had a problem which was solved in the end. Steve's story had a problem as well,

which wasn't solved at the end. You can see what I mean when I read them.'

When Mr Kerry had finished reading, everybody clapped wildly as Charlie went up to receive his prize – two terrific computer games!

'Three cheers for Charlie!' the school cried.

Charlie could hardly wait to get home and tell Mum and Dad the good news.

'I won the "write a story" competition!' he shouted.

There was no reply. Where could they all be?

He wandered upstairs to his bedroom, and there he had the surprise of his life. Standing on his table was a brand-new computer with a message on the screen –

TO CHARLIE.
AN EARLY PRESENT FOR YOUR
BIRTHDAY & CHRISTMAS.
LOVE,
UNCLE TIM.

'WHOOPEE!' he yelled.

Suddenly, he noticed a huge bulge in the curtains and out sprang Mum and Dad. At the same time, Mike and Josie wriggled from under the bed where they had been hiding.

Mum gave him a big hug.

'Well done, Charlie!' Dad beamed.

'We could hardly restrain ourselves when we heard you'd won the competition,' grinned Mike. 'But we wanted to see your face when you spotted your computer!'

'I can't wait to try it!' Charlie typed another sentence on the screen. 'What does this say, Josie?'

Josie studied it carefully and Mum whispered in her ear.

'Well,' – she took a deep breath and shouted –

'COMPUTER FOR CHARLIE! HURRAH! HURRAH!'

COUNTY ROVERS FOR CHARLIE

Chapter One

'HURRAH!' Charlie cried. 'We've arrived!'

The school bus lurched and bumped into Farmer Griffin's field, then came to a sudden halt.

'Whoops!' The boys shot forward and some fell out of their seats. Bert Coles picked himself up from the floor.

'Steady on, Mr Kerry!' he grumbled.

Mr Kerry breathed a sigh of relief.

'Sorry, chaps! If I drive in as far as I can, it's easier to unload.'

'All out!' shouted Mr Taylor. 'That is – except the boys sitting on the back row. I shall need them to carry the gear.'

A loud groan came from the rear.

'Now then! If you're lucky enough to come to summer camp, you have to help with the chores. There's washing up, setting tables and cleaning jobs. The duty list is pinned on the notice-board in the main hut. There's another list which tells you which bunk house you're in.'

A crowd of boys soon surrounded the notice-board.

Joe gave Titch a helpful push.

'Wriggle your way through to the front!' he suggested. 'Good job you're small!'

'Bunk house two!' Titch shouted seconds later. 'Here we are – Mac, Jason, Jake, Charlie, Joe, Bill, Bert, Trevor, Mick – but I'm not with you!' he cried.

'I'll swop!' offered Trevor kindly.

'Mr Stocks made out the bunk house list,' hissed Joe. 'He said we weren't to change.'

'Oh,' sighed Trevor. 'We'd better stay as we are.'

Titch's heart sank. He didn't want to be left out of the gang.

'I need helpers,' interrupted Mr Kerry. 'It will be getting dark soon, there's food boxes to unload, or we won't be getting any supper!'

Later that night, Titch slipped out of

the door at the back of his bunk house. The moon was bright above the trees and threw ghostly shadows across the grass. Half crouching, he ran as fast as he could. Out of the corner of his eye, he could see Mr Kerry sitting at a table outside the hut. He was drinking beer and playing cards with Mr Taylor and Mr Stocks.

At last he reached bunk house two, and before he opened the door, he covered his head with a handkerchief.

'Ghost!' he hissed, poking his head round.

There was a gasp of horror from the gang.

'Only a titchy ghost!' he chuckled.

'Good old Titch!' said Mac. 'Come and join us!'

'We're telling ghost stories,' explained Trevor, 'that's why you gave us such a shock!'

'Sit on my bunk,' offered Charlie. 'I bagged the bottom one. It's great! Joe's above me and when he snores, I give the mattress a shove and he stops at once!'

Titch curled up happily at the bottom

of Charlie's bunk. Jason was on guard as he was nearest the window.

'We're having football coaching first thing every morning,' Jake announced. 'I think Mr Taylor will choose Charlie or Bob Sharp for the County Rovers team.'

'Mr Taylor coaches loads of other schools,' said Titch.

'We're lucky to have him on our staff,' added Jake. 'He's super.'

'Bob's in my bunk house,' Titch groaned. 'Dave and Terry too. They're ganging up and bullying me already, just like they do at school. I expect it's because I'm small.'

'Don't take any notice,' advised Bill. 'They're never as tough as they pretend and they don't have any real friends. My Dad says so. He says you even get "grown-up" bullies.'

'Look out!' Jason hissed suddenly. 'Here's Mr Kerry doing his rounds.'

Titch shot out the back of the hut and only just managed to creep back to his own bunk house without being seen. He dived into his sleeping bag, and before he knew where he was he woke to the sound of a clanging bell.

'Breakfast time!' shouted Mr Kerry. 'Football starts straight after. Remember, Mr Taylor has come with us especially to choose a player for the County Rovers. Do your best!'

They ate breakfast on a long trestle table outside the kitchen hut.

'There's cereals and as much bread and marmalade as you want!' announced Joe. 'Help yourself to tea or milk.'

'We fetched the milk from the farm,' chorused Mick and Terry. 'Mr Griffin has the biggest bull you've ever seen. It has a ring in its nose and it snorted like mad at us!'

Charlie couldn't wait to finish breakfast. He was desperate to play well and be chosen for the County Rovers team.

Soon they were racing on to the field next to the farm-house.

'It makes a jolly good football pitch,' remarked Joe.

After training exercises, Bob Sharp was placed to play against Charlie. Bob was quick and defended well. It wasn't until the end of the game that Charlie

had his chance. Twisting and turning, he dribbled the ball towards goal. Bob tried desperately to stop him; he stuck his foot out trying to trip Charlie, but Charlie weaved to the side and avoided him.

'NOW SHOOT!' Mr Taylor yelled.

Charlie booted the ball with all his might. THWACK!

The ball just caught the side of the goal post and bounced back towards Bob. He was there in no time, and cleared it safely from the goal area.

'Well played, Bob!' encouraged Mr Taylor.

The whistle blew shrilly, and Charlie's heart sank.

'Hard luck, Charlie!' Titch sighed. 'Better luck next time.'

'Race you to the changing hut!' suggested Jason. 'I want to bag a canoe before they all get taken.'

'I'd rather fish for trout,' decided Joe. 'Mr Stocks is taking anyone who wants to fish out in the big motor boat.'

'We're going to barbecue the trout tonight,' said Bert. 'I heard Mr Stocks telling Mr Taylor.'

'WHOOPEE!' cried Jake. 'Let's get a move on!'

Chapter Two

'Oh no!' moaned Jason. 'There isn't a canoe left.'

'Bad luck!' grinned Bert. 'Titch and I grabbed the last one.'

'Come with us!' Charlie cried. 'Trout fishing is great! My Uncle Tim takes me in his boat sometimes.'

Mr Stocks started the engine. It spluttered and roared into action, blowing out clouds of smoke.

'PHEW!' Jason coughed. 'What a stink!'

Soon they were anchored upstream in calm waters and busy hauling in the trout.

'I've got a whopper here!' cried Jason. 'What fun!'

Charlie snatched the net and the trout was landed safely.

'I can see Bert and Titch in the distance,' remarked Joe.

Mr Stocks glanced up and frowned.

'It looks as though they're being chased,' he muttered.

'Yes, you're right. It's Bob Sharp and Dave, I think.' Joe squinted.

'COR!' Mick gasped. 'They've rammed Bert and Titch!'

'The canoe's upside down!' Charlie shouted. 'Bert's swimming in the water, but there's no sign of Titch!'

Mr Stocks wasted no time. He hauled up the anchor, started the engine and sped over to the scene of the accident.

'Grab hold of the boat, Bert!' he shouted, as he turned off the engine.

Mr Stocks dived into the river as he saw Titch's head appear, and swam towards him. Back at the camp, Mr Taylor had seen the canoe capsize and had raced along the river bank. He helped Mr Stocks pull Titch safely on to dry land.

Dripping wet, Bert and Titch were

taken back to the camp, none the worse for their ordeal.

Mr Kerry looked furious as he summoned them later on.

'Two boys did a very stupid thing today. Everyone knows it's dangerous to play about in boats, and ramming a canoe could have led to serious consequences. Bob Sharp and Dave Smith deserve to be sent home, but instead they'll miss the barbecue tonight and also have to clear up after it!'

Bob and Dave, red in the face, shuffled off to their bunk house.

'Good riddance!' chanted the boys, as they helped prepare for the barbecue.

And what a great success this was. They sat round the fire when they had eaten, drinking Coke and singing songs. Mr Kerry played his guitar, and even the farm cats came to listen.

'I bet they're really after the fish!' laughed Charlie.

At last, Mr Kerry couldn't be persuaded to play any more.

'We've a busy day tomorrow,' he said. 'A treasure hunt up the mountain, and a picnic when we reach the top.'

'Football game first!' Mr Taylor interrupted. 'So you'll need plenty of energy.'

'COR!' shouted Trevor. 'My legs are aching now!'

'Don't worry!' Mr Stocks comforted. 'You'll be sitting down in the evening. But that's a surprise!'

'Come on, Mr Stocks!' they all yelled. 'Tell us what it is!'

'Shall we tell them?' asked Mr Stocks.

'Oh! Go on, then!' laughed Mr Kerry. 'We have a screen and a projector to show you a . . . JAMES BOND FILM!'

'HURRAH!' The roar was deafening, and the farm cats twitched their ears and ran into the darkness.

'No more noise now,' hushed Mr Kerry. 'And sleep well!'

When they were getting changed into their football gear the next morning, Titch took Charlie on one side.

'Look out, Charlie!' warned Titch, in a low voice. 'There's been a lot of whispering going on between Bob, Dave and Terry.'

'What did they say?' Charlie frowned anxiously.

'I couldn't hear much. Something about "getting rid of that Charlie Lavender, so Bob could play for County Rovers".'

Charlie's heart sank. He thrust his foot into his sock angrily.

'OUCH!' he yelled, dragging off the sock as quickly as possible. 'Something sharp stuck in my toe.'

Charlie studied the sock carefully.

'It's a drawing pin!' he cried. 'And I think I know who put it there.'

There was a deathly silence in the changing hut.

Charlie went red with rage. He walked up to Bob and handed him the drawing pin.

'This belongs to you,' he said. 'And I think you are a stupid idiot.'

'I don't know what you're talking about,' Bob blustered.

'Then you're a liar as well!' retorted Charlie, as he walked away.

Mr Taylor appeared in the doorway.

'Tell him!' Titch hissed.

'It's no good,' sighed Charlie. 'He'd just think I was trying to get Bob into more trouble.'

'Get a move on!' urged Mr Taylor. 'Time you were outside!'

Chapter Three

Charlie didn't play very well. His toe was painful and hurt every time he ran.

'Come on, Charlie!' Mr Taylor shouted. 'Get a move on!'

Bob defended him all the time. He held and pushed Charlie at every opportunity. Mr Taylor didn't seem to notice.

At last the whistle blew.

'Collect your picnic from the kitchen hut. We leave for the treasure hunt in twenty minutes.'

Charlie limped off the field.

'What's the matter with you?' asked Titch.

'My toe hurts!' Charlie explained miserably.

'You can have one of my plasters,' Joe offered. 'Mum insisted on putting some in. She said we'd be bound to get a few blisters!'

The plaster made all the difference. Charlie was soon tramping up the mountain with Titch and Joe, able to enjoy the treasure hunt.

'What was the last clue?' Titch panted.

Thunder and lightning strikes.
It holds the key to open the door.

They hurried on, the bracken crunching under their feet.

'THAT'S IT!' pointed Joe. 'A tree which has been struck by lightning!'

Sure enough, a note was nailed to the dead bark.

Climb the rocks to the left.
The door needs no key.
But shelter is there
and so is the end of the trail.

The three boys did just as the note instructed.

'Hurrah!' cried Charlie as they clambered over the rocks. 'There's Mr Stocks sitting outside a cave.'

'Jason and Trevor are eating their picnic.' Joe's mouth watered. 'I'm famished!'

'Well done, you three!' Mr Stocks grinned. 'You're not quite the first, but there's lots behind you.'

They flung themselves down thankfully, and set about eating.

The others arrived in twos and threes, and soon the mountain echoed with their laughter.

'I feel as though I'm on top of the world!' said Jake.

'Make the most of it,' laughed Mr Kerry. 'I'll give you half an hour to explore before the descent. When you hear the whistle head back for camp.'

The boys scattered everywhere.

'I've found another cave!' Joe shouted.

Charlie and Titch ran to join him.

'It's very creepy!' shuddered Titch. 'I can't see a thing.'

'Your eyes will soon get used to the dark,' said Joe bravely.

'PHEW!' Charlie held his nose. 'What a stink!'

Suddenly, there was a ghost-like moan and they clutched each other, trembling.

'I can see shadowy things,' whispered Joe.

'I'm s-s-s-scared!' Titch stuttered.

'Me too!' agreed Charlie.

'WHOOOO! WHOOOO!' The sound grew louder.

They stood frozen to the spot.

Suddenly, there was a burst of laughter. The shadows moved and became human shapes.

'It's Jason and Bill!' shouted Charlie. 'You rotten things!'

Laughing, they chased them out of the cave.

'We'll get you!' Titch yelled.

Just then, the whistle blew shrilly and reluctantly they began the journey back.

'Good job it's downhill,' groaned Jason. 'My legs will hardly carry me.'

*

That night, they collapsed thankfully to watch the James Bond film. Mr Kerry had quite a job to quieten the thunderous applause when it ended.

'What a great film!' Titch yawned as he slid down later into his sleeping bag.

Moments later, he let out a terrible scream.

'EEEEK! There's a creepy-crawly in my bed!'

Titch unzipped the bag to see three huge spiders scuttling away. There was

a loud guffaw from Bob, Terry and Dave.

'You rotters!' shouted Titch.

'BE QUIET!' stormed Mr Kerry appearing at the doorway. 'GO TO SLEEP AT ONCE!'

No one dared say anything after that. Lying in the dark, Titch felt miserable. It was all very well for Bill to say ignore Bob, Dave and Terry, but that was hard to do when they put spiders in your sleeping bag.

Tired out and wishing he was with

his friends in the other bunk house, Titch fell asleep.

The groans could be heard all over the camp next morning.

'My joints need oiling!' complained Bill. 'I can hardly move!'

'The quicker you get going the better you'll be,' laughed Mr Kerry. 'I've had to ring the bell especially loud today.'

'Stop moaning!' Mr Taylor grumbled. 'Plenty of limbering up exercises before the football game will soon put you right.'

Charlie couldn't find his boots anywhere.

'Hasn't anyone seen them?' Charlie asked desperately.

'You can't play without them, can you?' sneered Terry.

'You'll never find them!' taunted Bob.

'This time we're making sure you won't be chosen for the Rovers.'

'It's you lot!' Charlie gasped. 'I might have known.'

'Tell us where you've hidden them!' Titch raged.

Mr Taylor appeared in the doorway.

'HURRY UP!' he cried. 'What a lot of slow coaches.'

'Please! – I can't find –' began Charlie. But Mr Taylor disappeared and so had everyone else.

All except Titch, who handed his boots to Charlie.

'Borrow mine!' he offered. 'I shall never be chosen to play for the Rovers.'

'Thanks, Titch!'

Charlie thrust his foot in one.

'It's no good!' he wailed. 'They're too small.'

'SHUSH! What's that?' Titch listened carefully.

‘There’s a scuffling sound over there,’ replied Charlie, wheeling round.

‘Look! It’s the farm cat!’ exclaimed Titch. ‘He’s after a mouse. It ran in the corner behind the shelves.’

The cat pounced. There was a loud crash as the shelves toppled over. Balls rolled everywhere. Life jackets, skittles, ropes, fishing rods were scattered about. And there, on top, were a pair of black and white football boots!

‘MY BOOTS!’ cried Charlie. ‘They hid them behind the shelves!’

Charlie and Titch raced on to the field just in time for the kick-off. It was raining hard and very muddy. They were slipping and sliding everywhere.

Bob, Dave and Terry were very sur-

prised to see Charlie run on to the pitch. Charlie gave them a scornful look. He was so angry at their dirty tricks to keep him out of the game, that it made him more determined to show them all how well he could play.

Jason dribbled the ball to Charlie.

'Here's my chance,' thought Charlie.

Glancing up, he saw Bob hovering in front of him, waiting to intercept.

Charlie dodged to the side and overtook him at a tremendous speed. His anger spurred him on to super-human efforts and he tore up the field like a tornado.

There was a great thwack as his boot struck the ball. It shot through the air like a bullet and landed in the middle of the goal posts. The goalkeeper was left lying spreadeagled in the mud.

The roar was deafening.

'GOAL!' they yelled. 'Good old Charlie!'

In the second half, Terry missed a pass and Bob Sharp intercepted. His feet shot from under him and he fell heavily with a cry.

A crowd gathered round him. Mr Taylor took Bob's boot off very gently, and rolled down his sock.

'I'm afraid it's a bad strain,' Mr Taylor said. 'Luckily, it's not broken. I'm afraid you'll be out of action for some time.'

'Serves him right,' whispered Titch. 'My Mum says you get paid back if you do something nasty!'

Mr Stocks helped Mr Taylor carry Bob off the field.

Mr Taylor was soon back. 'Accidents will happen!' he said. 'Now let's get on with the game.'

Charlie played all out for the remainder of the time. He was pleased with his efforts, but he knew how well Bob had played in all the games before he was injured.

Who would Mr Taylor pick for the County Rovers team? Nobody could be sure.

In a few weeks Bob's sprained ankle would be as good as new. Ah, well, it wouldn't be long before they had the answer.

Later on, Titch joined the gang in the last night midnight feast.

'Just think!' Charlie said. 'I nearly

missed summer camp this year.'

'Were you going to do something else?' asked Trevor.

'My Dad said I couldn't come because I'd been disobedient,' explained Charlie.

'He thought Charlie had fiddled with his office computer,' interrupted Joe. 'It was his sister, Josie!'

'But it took a long time before he realized it wasn't me!'

Charlie took the last swig from his can of ginger beer and choked noisily.

'Shut up!' Jason hissed. 'It's Mr Kerry, and he's coming here!'

There was a desperate scramble to hide the debris and dive into sleeping bags. Titch wriggled under Charlie's bunk but got stuck half-way.

'Your feet are sticking out!' cried Charlie.

Mr Kerry flung open the door and held the lamp high.

'Bit noisy in here! But as it's the last night, I'll turn a blind eye.'

He gave a huge wink and the gang cheered loudly.

'Good news for you, Charlie,' Mr Kerry grinned. 'Mr Taylor has chosen you to join the County Rovers!'

'Wow!' Charlie gasped. 'Aren't I lucky!'

'Three cheers for Charlie! HIP! HIP! HURRAH!'